BEN M. BAGLIO

The Playful Puppy

Illustrated by
Andy Ellis

D0288548

A
LITTLE APPLE
PAPERBACK

SCHOLASTIC INC.

New York Toronto London Auckland Sydney
Mexico City New Delhi Hong Kong Buenos Aires

ISBN 0-439-41914-X

Text copyright © 2001 by Working Partners Limited.
Original series created by Ben M. Baglio.
Illustrations copyright © 2001 by Andy Ellis.

12 11 10 9 8 7 6 5 4 3 2 1   2 3 4 5 6 7/0

Printed in the U.S.A.   40
First Scholastic printing, September 2002

To Sophie and Benjamin — two cairn terriers
that were the best little pals in the world

Special thanks to Narinder Dhami

1

"I'm going to third grade!" Mandy Hope sang as she clattered down the stairs.

"Breakfast first, Mandy," said her mom, Emily Hope, smiling. "You've got a busy day ahead of you."

It was the first day of school. Mandy had been longing for today to arrive. She was moving up from second grade to third grade!

But there was another reason for being excited . . .

Her friend Peter Foster had picked up his new cairn terrier puppy last night. And Peter had said that he and his mom would be bringing the puppy to school with them this morning!

Mandy loved animals, which was a good thing, because there were always lots of them at home!

Her mom and dad were vets. Their clinic, Animal Ark, was at the back of their house, in the village of Welford.

Mandy didn't have any pets of her own, though. Animal Ark

was busy enough! But her friends' pets were the next best thing.

Adam Hope, Mandy's dad, came into the kitchen. He laughed as Mandy tried to eat her cornflakes as fast as she could.

"Slow down, there's plenty of time," he said. "I'm taking you to school today. Mom's on Animal Ark duty."

Dr. Emily pulled on her white coat and gave Mandy a quick hug. "Have a good day, dear," she said. "See you later." Then she hurried into the Animal Ark clinic.

Mandy got up and put her empty bowl in the sink. "Finished! Can we go now, please, Dad?"

Mandy could hardly sit still as her father drove through Welford.

She was surprised when her dad stopped the Land Rover outside the second-grade entrance at Welford Village School. "What are you doing, Dad?" she asked.

"I'm not in second grade anymore — I'm in third grade now!"

"I'm sorry, Mandy," said Dr. Adam. "I forgot." Then he winked at her.

"Oh, *Dad!*" Mandy laughed.

Dr. Adam drove a little farther on, to the third-grade door.

Mandy looked through the

railings at the big third-grade playground. She was excited but a little scared, too.

She soon cheered up, though, when she saw Peter and Mrs. Foster at the school door. Peter was holding a tiny bundle of sandy-colored fur in his arms.

"Look, Dad," Mandy said breathlessly. "There's Peter's new puppy!"

She climbed out of the car and rushed over.

"Hi, Mandy!" Peter called. He smiled widely as he spotted his friend. "Come and say hello to Timmy!"

The puppy looked up at Mandy with dark, shining eyes.

He gave a little woof and wagged his short stumpy tail.

Mandy thought Timmy was *wonderful.* He was small but sturdy, and his fluffy coat was pale brown, except for dark smudges on his face. And he had sweet ears that flopped over at the corners.

"Hello, Timmy," Mandy said. She gently stroked the puppy's head. Timmy sniffed her hand, and then licked it with his little pink tongue. "Oh, Peter, he's so cute!"

"He certainly is," agreed Dr. Adam, after he had parked the car and joined Mandy. "Hello, boy!"

Peter grinned proudly. "Do

you want to hold him, Mandy?"
he asked.

"Oh, can I?" Mandy gasped.

Peter handed Timmy over.
The puppy didn't seem to mind,
and he cuddled happily in
Mandy's arms.

She held him carefully, loving
the feel of Timmy's solid, warm
body.

As Mandy rubbed her cheek against his soft fur, Timmy sniffed her ear, then gave her a big, wet lick on the nose.

"Did you take him for a walk this morning, Peter?" Mandy asked.

"No, Timmy's only eight weeks old," Peter said. "He has to have more shots before he's allowed to walk around outside. Until then, we have to carry him everywhere."

Dr. Adam nodded. "Timmy will come to Animal Ark for his shots in four weeks, Mandy," he said. "You know why they are so important, don't you?"

Mandy nodded. "They will help stop Timmy from catching illnesses from outside," she said.

"That's right," her dad agreed. "After his shots, Timmy will be able to go for walks safely."

"Mom, can Mandy come to

our house after school?" Peter asked.

"Yes, of course, if Dr. Adam agrees," Mrs. Foster said, smiling.

"Can I, please, Dad?" Mandy asked eagerly.

"Of course, you can, dear," Dr. Adam told her. "There's the bell. Off you go, now."

Mandy gave Timmy a last cuddle and handed him over to Peter's mom. Then she followed Peter into the big third-grade playground.

2

Mandy opened her new writing
book to the first page.
Her first day in third
grade had been fun,
so far. Mandy was
at the same table
as Peter, which was
great! And their
new teacher, Ms.
Rushton, seemed
very friendly.

"Put the date at the top of the page, please," Ms. Rushton told them. "Now I want to hear all about what you did over the summer. And I want to see some nice pictures, too," she added.

Mandy thought for a while and then decided to write about the day her grandma and grandpa took her to the seashore. As she picked up her pencil, she glanced across at Peter. He'd already started writing. Mandy leaned over to read it.

I got my new puppy, Timmy, last night. He's a cairn terrier, and he's great. I played with him a little. Then he went to sleep. Mom says puppies need to rest a lot, but I hope Timmy doesn't sleep <u>all</u> the time!

Peter was now drawing a picture of his puppy, curled up asleep.

Mandy smiled. Timmy was so cute. She couldn't wait until school was over, so she could see him again!

"Look, Peter, there they are!"
Mandy said. She and Peter raced
across the playground toward
Mrs. Foster, who was waiting at
the door with Timmy.

Mandy had enjoyed her first
day in third grade. Ms. Rushton

had talked about all the new things they were going to do. But now it was time to play with Timmy!

"Hi, Mom, hi, Timmy!" Peter beamed as he took the pup and gave him a cuddle. "Did you miss me, boy?"

Mandy laughed. Timmy was bouncing up and down in Peter's arms and licking his owner's nose, with little yelps of delight. "Yes, I think he missed you!" she said. She scratched the top of Timmy's head. Timmy turned around and gave her a little lick, too.

"Come on, let's go home," Mrs. Foster said, smiling.

They set off down the street. When they reached the corner, Peter turned to Mandy.

"Would you like to carry Timmy for a while?" he asked.

"Oh, yes, please!" Mandy said.

Timmy snuggled down into Mandy's arms. He seemed happy to be carried, although he sat up and had a good look when a man with a German shepherd dog went by.

"No, Timmy," Mandy told him. "That dog's too big for you to play with!"

"Ruff!" Timmy replied, smiling, and licked Mandy's cheek.

When they got home, Peter and Mandy took Timmy into the living room.

Mandy was hoping that Timmy would want to play. But the puppy ran behind the sofa and didn't come back out.

"What are you doing, Timmy?" Peter asked, bending down to take a look.

"That's his favorite place to sleep at the moment," Mrs. Foster said, coming in from the kitchen. "He's been behind there all day."

Mandy knelt down at the other end of the sofa to look. "I don't think he's asleep," she said. "I think he's chewing something!"

"What?" Mrs. Foster frowned and quickly pulled the sofa away from the wall.

Timmy was having a wonderful time chewing a very bright-colored and very soggy piece of material. He wagged his tail happily at everyone.

"Oh, no! That's your father's new tie, Peter!" Mrs. Foster cried. "Grandma gave him that!" She tried to grab the tie from Timmy, but the puppy didn't want to let go. He hung on tightly, playing tug-of-war.

On her hands and knees, Mandy crept up behind Timmy. She leaned over the pup and gently pulled the tie from his tiny jaws.

Still playing, Timmy turned around and pounced on Mandy's lap. Mandy tried not to laugh. She held the tie out of Timmy's reach and handed it over to Mrs. Foster.

Mandy thought it was the most awful tie she'd ever seen. It was bright green with purple and orange flowers all over it.

"Dad hates that tie!" Peter grinned at his mom. "And so do you!"

Mrs. Foster laughed. "Yes, all right," she agreed. "But Timmy still shouldn't have chewed it."

They all looked at Timmy. He was tired out from all the excitement and gave a big yawn. Then he lay down and curled up in a furry little ball to go to sleep.

"Oh, Timmy!" Mrs. Foster said, shaking her head. "That was *very* naughty!"

But Mandy saw that she was smiling.

3

"Mom, Timmy's so cute!" Mandy said happily. "I can't wait for you to see him."

It was the next morning. Dr. Emily was taking Mandy to school today.

But when they arrived at the school door, Mandy was very disappointed. Timmy, Peter, and Mrs. Foster were nowhere to be seen.

"Sorry, dear," Dr. Emily said. "I must go, or I'll be late for my visit to Mrs. Dawkins. One of her ponies is very sick. I'll see Timmy another time, OK?"

"OK," Mandy said, waving good-bye as her mom drove off. Then she went into the playground and waited near the gate. Perhaps Peter was sick and wasn't coming to school today.

Then, just a few minutes before the bell, Mandy saw Peter and Mrs. Foster rushing toward the door. Peter's mom had Timmy in her arms.

"Oh, Mandy, guess what happened!" Peter panted. "Timmy chewed my dad's shoelaces so much that when he went to put his shoes on, the laces fell to pieces!"

"That's why we're so late," Mrs. Foster explained. "We had to hunt around the house for another pair."

Timmy wagged his tail, not looking at all ashamed of himself.

"Oh, Timmy!" Mandy said.

"Mom, did I put my reading book in my bag?" Peter asked, trying to pull his backpack off. "I can't remember."

"Let me look," Mrs. Foster

said. "Mandy, will you hold Timmy for me?"

Mandy nodded eagerly and took Timmy in her arms. Right away, the puppy tried to chew Mandy's hair.

"No, Timmy," Mandy said, shaking her hair back out of the puppy's reach. "Dogs don't eat hair!"

Timmy gave a little bark, as if he was surprised to hear that. He turned his attention to the neck of Mandy's school sweatshirt instead.

"Oh, Timmy!" Mrs. Foster sighed as she looked through Peter's backpack. "Can't you *ever* stop chewing things?"

As Mandy gently pushed Timmy's mouth away from the neck of her sweatshirt, he started to chew her fingers. Mandy couldn't help laughing.

"Is my book there, Mom?" Peter asked anxiously. "Ms. Rushton said we had to bring them back today."

"Yes, it's here," Mrs. Foster

replied, pulling the book out. "Oh, no!"

Mandy, Peter, and Mrs. Foster stared at the book. One corner of it had been chewed, and there were tiny teeth marks on the glossy cover.

"I didn't notice that when I put it in my bag because I was in such a rush." Peter groaned. "Oh, Timmy!"

"Tell Ms. Rushton we'll pay for it," Mrs. Foster said, looking a little annoyed now. "And, Timmy, stop chewing Mandy's fingers!"

The bell rang, and Mandy

gave Timmy back to Peter's mom. She hoped that Mrs. Foster wasn't *too* angry at Timmy.

4

After assembly, Ms. Rushton showed her class lots of pictures. They talked about the people in them. And then Ms. Rushton said, "Now I'd like you to write about *your* home."

Mandy wrote about Animal Ark and all the pets that visited with their owners. Then she leaned over to see what Peter had written. He'd gone to sharpen his pencil, but Mandy knew he wouldn't mind her looking. . . .

I live on Church Lane with my mom and dad and my new puppy, Timmy. His favorite things are sleeping and chewing. So far he's chewed Dad's new tie, Mom's purse, my pencil case, the bath mat, Dad's shoelaces, and my reading book.

Mandy looked at Peter's pencil case. Sure enough, there were tiny teeth marks on the corner.

"It will be playtime in five minutes, class," Ms. Rushton called. "Try to finish your work."

Quickly, Mandy picked up her pencil again, but she couldn't help feeling a little worried. Timmy's chewing could get him into big trouble. . . .

When they got to the playground a few minutes later, Peter said that he didn't feel like playing. Mandy offered him half of her cookies to cheer him up.

"Thanks," Peter said,
managing a small smile.

"Are you worried about
Timmy chewing things?" Mandy
asked.

Peter nodded and looked
miserable. "Dad was mad about
his tie being chewed — and *really*
mad when his laces fell to pieces

this morning. But chewing is just a game to Timmy," he said.

"We'll have to think of a less naughty game for him to play, then," Mandy said. She put the empty cookie wrapper in the playground trash can. Then she crossed her fingers for luck.

When the bell rang at the end of the day, Mandy and Peter hurried out into the playground. Mandy was going home with Peter again, for an early supper — and to play with Timmy, of course!

Peter's mom was waiting at the door with Timmy in her arms. The puppy looked very pleased to

see them. He barked a loud hello,
his tail wagging wildly.

"Have you been good today,
Timmy?" Peter asked nervously, as
he took the pup from his mom.

"He's been *very* good," Mrs.
Foster said, smiling, as they
walked along.

Mandy and Peter sighed with relief.

"Good boy!" Mandy said, scratching Timmy's sweet little ears. Timmy wagged his tail harder and licked her hand.

"He hasn't chewed anything he shouldn't — because I had a really good idea," said Mrs. Foster.

Mandy and Peter looked up at her, interested.

"You know those old red slippers that don't fit you anymore, Peter?" Mrs. Foster continued. "Well, I gave them to Timmy! I thought that if he had something of his own to chew, he might stop chewing everything

else. And it seems to have
worked!" she said.

"That's great, Mom!" said
Peter happily.

They soon reached home.

"All right, I'll go and make
our dinner," Mrs. Foster said.

Peter put Timmy down on the
floor and he bounded off into the
living room.

He came back, carrying an old red slipper in his mouth. He showed it to Mandy, looking very pleased with himself.

"Oh, is that your new toy, Timmy? It's wonderful!" Mandy said, laughing.

It certainly looked as if Mrs. Foster's idea had done the trick!

5

"I think we've tired Timmy out!" Mandy grinned, as the little pup gave a big yawn.

They'd been playing tug-of-war with Timmy and his slippers for almost half an hour. But now Timmy was stretched out on the rug, his eyes closed and his head between his paws.

"Dinnertime!" Peter's mom called from the kitchen.

"You have a nice snooze, Timmy," Peter whispered.

He grinned at Mandy, and they both tiptoed out to the kitchen.

Mrs. Foster had made fish sticks, french fries, and peas — and there was lemon-drizzle cake and milk for dessert.

Mandy ate as quickly as she could. She wanted to play with

Timmy again before her dad came to pick her up.

Peter ate even more quickly than Mandy. "Let's go and see if Timmy's awake," he said when he'd finished.

Mandy nodded eagerly. She crammed the last bite of cake into her mouth, then took her plate over to the sink. "Thanks, Mrs. Foster," she said. "That was great!" Then she hurried after Peter.

In the living room, one of Timmy's slippers lay on the rug and the other was behind an armchair. But there was no sign of Timmy.

"Timmy!" Peter called. "Where are you?"

Then, suddenly, there was a sound from upstairs.

"What's that noise?" Mrs. Foster said, coming out of the kitchen. "Where's Timmy?"

Feeling very worried, Mandy quickly followed Peter and his mom upstairs. What was Timmy up to?

Timmy was lying on the landing, concentrating very hard. He was trying to get his tiny jaw around the heel of a shiny new shoe. The other new shoe lay nearby. And its toe was covered with tiny teeth marks. . . .

Mandy's heart sank.

"Oh, *Timmy*!" Peter groaned.
"Those are my new school shoes!"

"Timmy!" Mrs. Foster gasped
furiously. "Those shoes were very
expensive! You bad dog!"

Timmy's ears went down, and
he began to whimper. He knew
he'd done something wrong.

Mandy felt so sorry for him.

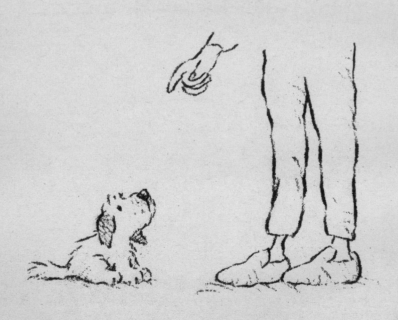

"He didn't mean it, Mom," Peter said miserably, picking up his pet.

But Mrs. Foster shook her head. "Bring Timmy downstairs, Peter," she snapped. "This is just too much!"

Now Mandy felt very worried. Timmy had gone too far this time, and Mrs. Foster was *really* angry.

6

Before Peter's mom could say anything else, the doorbell rang. It was Mandy's dad.

"Hello there, Mrs. Foster," Dr. Adam said, smiling. "I've come to take Mandy home —" Then he stopped as he saw how miserable everyone looked. "Is anything wrong?" he asked.

"Timmy's been very naughty," Mrs. Foster said crossly.

"He's chewed Peter's school shoes — and they were brand new!"

"Well, I'm afraid that you can't stop puppies from chewing things," Mandy's dad said. "They need to chew, because they're teething — just like human

babies! And sometimes they chew things they shouldn't."

"Mom gave Timmy my old slippers to chew, Dr. Adam," said Peter. "And it stopped him chewing *some* other things . . . but then he went and chewed my school shoes!"

Mandy looked anxiously at her dad. Would he be able to help Timmy?

"Well, it's not really Timmy's fault," said Dr. Adam calmly. "You see, he was given permission to chew your old slippers, Peter. Now Timmy thinks he can chew *anything* that smells the same, and he won't get into trouble."

"Oh!" Peter gasped. "I never thought of that."

"Oh, dear — then it's my fault," said Mrs. Foster. "It was my idea to give Timmy the slippers."

Dr. Adam looked at Peter and Mandy. Then he smiled. "I think we can work this out very easily.

Come on, you two. We're going for a drive — and let's take Timmy, too!"

Dr. Adam drove out of Welford to the nearby town of Walton. He stopped outside the local pet shop, Piper's Pets.

"Your mom *was* right, Peter," Dr. Adam said, as they all climbed out of the Land Rover. "Timmy does need his own things to chew. But they've got to be the right *kind* of things."

"You mean dog chews, Dad!" Mandy guessed.

Dr. Adam nodded. "That's right, Mandy. Dog chews will help Timmy's teeth to be healthy and strong," he said, pushing open the pet-shop door. "They're much better for him than slippers!"

Piper's Pets had lots of different dog chews to choose from. There were all sorts of colors, shapes, and sizes. Timmy

got very excited with all the interesting smells.

"These chews are perfect for Timmy," Dr. Adam said, picking up some chunky sticks and some thin strips. "And they will taste a lot nicer to him than old slippers and new school shoes!"

"I think Timmy agrees with you, Dr. Adam!" said Peter, grinning. Timmy was leaning over, trying to steal one of the chews from Dr. Adam's hand.

"Make sure that you give Timmy lots of praise when he chews something he's supposed to, Peter," Dr. Adam advised, as he paid for the chews.

Peter nodded. "I will. Thanks, Dr. Adam!"

Mandy was glad to see that Peter looked much happier. Thank goodness her dad knew what to do! She just hoped Timmy would behave himself from now on.

"Timmy's finished the chews your dad bought him, Mandy," Peter said, a week later.

He and Mandy were in the Fosters' living room watching TV. They had been playing with Timmy, but now the puppy was in the kitchen, eating his dinner. "Timmy really loves them. But they only lasted a week!"

"Well, they stopped him from chewing things he shouldn't, didn't they?" Mandy asked.

Peter nodded. But before he could say anything else, there was a shout from the kitchen.

"Timmy!" Mrs. Foster called. "Don't you dare!"

Peter and Mandy ran to the door. They were just in time to see Timmy dash through the open kitchen door and out into the yard. He was trailing a blue-and-white tea towel behind him, like a flag.

"Timmy!" Mrs. Foster yelled

as she ran out of the kitchen after him. "Bring that back!"

"I think it's time to get Timmy some more chews!" Mandy grinned as she and Peter ran to join in the chase.